55 WAVERLY STREET

55 WAVERLY STREET

by **Thom Black**   *with* Lynda Stephenson
illustrated by **Mary Chambers**

ZondervanPublishingHouse
Grand Rapids, Michigan

A Division of HarperCollinsPublishers

55 Waverly Street
Text copyright © 1998 by Family University, LLC
Illustrations copyright © 1998 by Family University, LLC

Requests for information should be addressed to:
ZondervanPublishingHouse
Grand Rapids, Michigan 49530

Library of Congress Cataloging-in-Publication Data

Black, Thom.
    55 Waverly Street / by Thom Black ; illustrated by Mary Chambers.
        p.   cm.
    Summary: A little boy finds a special place where he does what his heart wants, and when he grows up,
he searches once again for the meaningful place of his childhood.
    ISBN 0-310-20792-4 (hc)
    [1. Imagination—Fiction. 2. Stories in rhyme.]   I. Chambers, Mary, ill.   II. Title.
    PZ8.3.B572Aae   1998
    [E]—dc21
                                                 97-34061
                                                   CIP
                                                    AC

This edition printed on acid-free paper and meets the American National Standards Institute Z39.48 standard.

Printed in Mexico

98 99 00 01 02 03 /❖ DR/ 10 9 8 7 6 5 4 3 2 1

I have seen the burden God has laid on men....
He has also set eternity in the hearts of men.
—Ecclesiastes

There is a house down the street
that's always been there.
With two stories (and possibly more).
With hedges so high tippytoes can't see over, and . . .

... hedge holes just big enough to slip through.
Where children up the street disappear to.

To do what they do, do, do.

There was a boy who lived on the street.
He loved the house
and what he did there.

And he thought he would always go there.

But one day he was told of other plans planned for him.
He had to get bigger, that was the rule.
And bigger, bigger, bigger he grew.
And busier with school
and a thousand, thousand, thousand things
he "must" do.

Until he was too big for the house and its hedge hole.
Too busy to remember quite where it was, in fact.
Left at the corner? Around the back?
He was too busy even to think about that.

And after a while, he didn't much think of it,
had hardly a thought of it,
nary a memory of it.
Except now and then,
when the moment was his own,

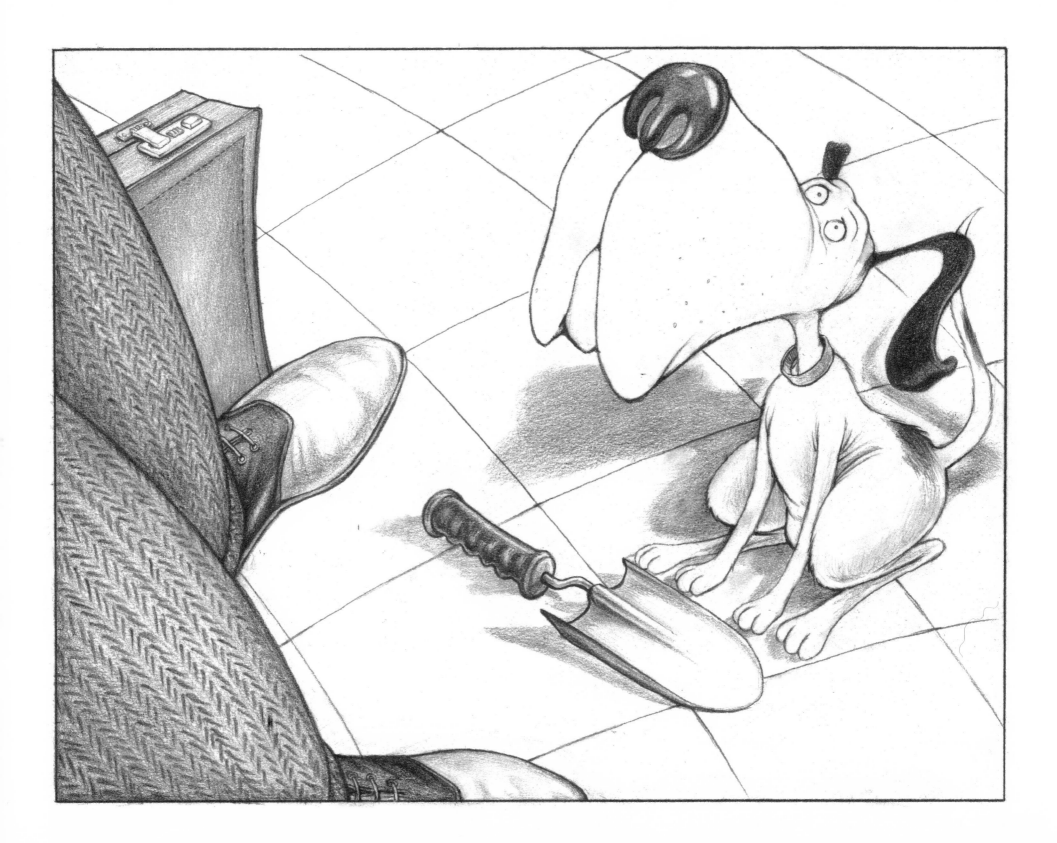

and all was quiet.

And so it goes, and so it went.
The boy got as big, bigger, biggest as he could get
—and as busy as required.
Until one night he was just plain tired.
He had done all he could, he had done what he must.
He could do no more.
No more!
He sighed.

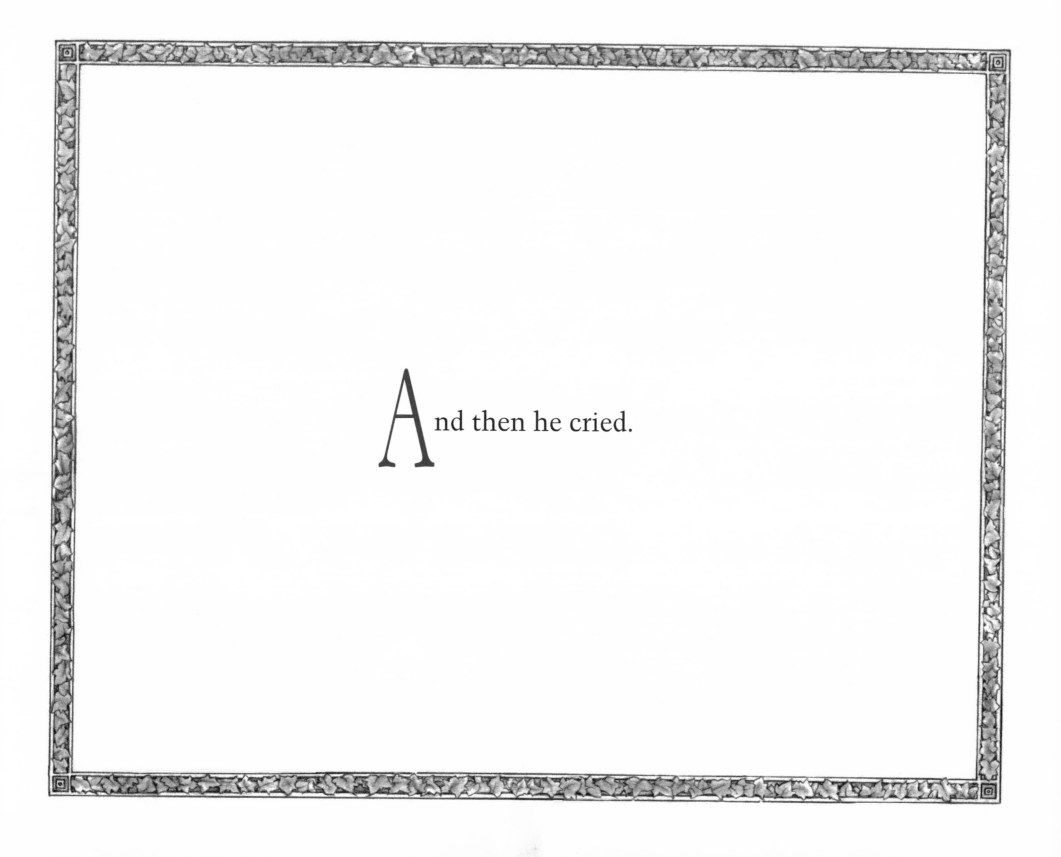

And then he cried.

So late that evening,
when the moon woke him from sleep,
he got to his feet.
And he started walking, walking,
walking down the street.

Left he went, then right—
wandering forlornly this way and that
until he saw a place faintly familiar.

A house with two big stories (and possibly more).
With hedges so high tippytoes can't see over,
but with holes just big enough to skinny through.
Where—why, yes—children of his street
once disappeared to.

And in the moon's glow he bent down to see
the hole he once squeezed through so easily.
Now, though, he could never get through.
So the boy grown big turned to go.

Until he saw something new.

From the hole reached a hand, reached right to him!
So gingerly, carefully, cautiously, he took it.
And he was pulled into the hedge …

. . . and through it . . .

. . . back into the big house's yard and into the sunlight.

"Where have you been?"
A girl had hold of his hand.
And the boy grown old noticed he was back little again.
"No one can fix plants like you!"
And she held out a flower pot cracked clear through.

The big little boy felt his heart swell.
This was the place,
the place to do what you were always meant to do,
now he knew it.
Because there were his old sign, his dirt and his plants,
and a long line of friends waiting for him just to do it.

So, dirt flying,
hands dancing with glee,
the boy fixed one plant, then two and three.
He remembered now,
he remembered anew,
what God had designed him so well,
so wondrously always to do.

Then he noticed the sign hanging on the next tree.
His eyes grew big, his heart swelling bigger.
He jumped to his feet and
slipped back through the hedge hole.
Not a moment to waste.
Someone he knew belonged here as well.
Someone he must bring here,
to this secret place.

To the house down the street with two stories (and many more).
Where we can finally, always,
forever do what was placed in our heart,
stamped on our soul,
designed in our being—
the thing we were meant for.